my black hen
lays eggs

This is the cock that crowed in the morn

CHICKENS ARE ROOSTING IN THE BARN

NOTES

Notes & Numbers

Personal Notes

Name ....

Address ....

....

....

Tel.: Home ....

Business ....

Car ....

In Case of Emergency

Contact ....

Telephone No. ....

Blood Group ....

Known Allergies ....

Useful Information

eg. Passport Details, Car Information etc

....

....

....

....

....

....

....

....

....

....

....

Notes & Numbers

Useful Telephone Numbers

Accountant

Airport

Bank

Building Society

Club

Dentist

Doctor

Electrician

Gas

Optician

Plumber

Railway Station

Solicitor

Taxi/Car Hire

Travel Agent

Vet

Water

Others

Metric Information

Length

1 centimetre (cm)		= 0.3937 in
1 metre (m)	= 100 cm	= 1.0936 yds
1 kilometre (km)	= 1000 m	= 0.6214 mile
1 inch		= 2.5400 cm
1 yard	= 36 in	= 0.9144 m
1 mile	= 1760 yds	= 1.6093 km

Weight

1 gramme (g)	= 1000 mg	= 0.3535 oz
1 kilogramme (kg)	= 1000 g	= 2.2046 lb
1 tonne (t)	= 1000 kg	= 0.9842 ton
1 ounce	= 437.5 grains	= 28.350 g
1 pound	= 16 oz	= 0.4536 kg
1 ton	= 2240 pounds	= 1.0161 tonnes

Capacity

1 cu dm (dm³)	= 1000 cm³	= 0.0353 cu ft
1 cu metre (m³)	= 1000 dm³	= 1.3080 cu yds
1 litre	= 1 dm³	= 0.2200 gallon
1 cu yd	= 27 cu ft	= 0.7646 m³
1 pint	= 4 gills	= 0.5683 litre
1 gallon	= 8 pints	= 4.5461 litres

Area

1 sq metre (m²)	= 10 000 cm²	= 1.1960 sq yds
1 hectare (ha)	= 10 000 m²	= 2.4711 acres
1 sq km (km²)	= 100 hectares	= 0.3861 sq mile
1 sq yd	= 9 sq ft	= 0.8361 m²
1 acre	= 4840 sq yds	= 4046.9 m²

Metric Conversions

	multiply by
acres to hectares	0.4047
cubic inches to cubic centimetres	16.39
cubic feet to cubic metres	0.02832
cubic yards to cubic metres	0.7646
cubic inches to litres	0.01639
feet to metres	0.3048
gallons to litres	4.546
grains to grammes	0.0648
inches to centimetres	2.540
miles to kilometres	1.609

Metric Conversions

	multiply by
ounces to grammes	28.35
pounds to kilogrammes	0.4536
pounds to grammes	453.6
square inches to square centimetres	6.452
square feet to square metres	0.0929
square yards to square metres	0.8361
square miles to square kilometres	2.590
tons to kilogrammes	1016.00
yards to metres	0.9144

Speed

M.P.H.	20	30	40	50	60	70	80	90	100
K.P.H.	32	48	64	80	96	112	128	144	160

Tyre Pressures

lb per sq in	20	22	24	26	28	30	32	34
kg per sq cm	1.40	1.54	1.68	1.82	1.96	2.10	2.24	2.39

Fuel

Gallons	1	2	3	4	5
Litres	4.55	9.09	13.64	18.18	22.73
Gallons	6	7	8	9	10
Litres	27.28	31.82	36.37	40.91	45.46

Distance

Miles	1	5	10	25	30
Kilometres	1.61	8.05	16.09	40.23	80.47
Miles		75	100	250	500
Kilometres		120.70	160.90	402.27	804.70

Temperature

Fahrenheit	22°F	32°F	41°F	59°F	68°F	86°F
Celsius	-5°C	0°C	5°C	15°C	20°C	30°C

Cooking (Dial Markings)

Gasmark	¼	1	2	3	4	5	6	7	8	9
Fahrenheit	250	275	300	325	350	375	400	425	450	475
Celsius	120	140	150	160	180	190	200	220	230	240

Conversion Formulae

$$C = \frac{5}{9}(F-32) \qquad F = \frac{9}{5}(C+32)$$

Notes

FRUITS of the forest

rip

FRUIT

APPLES HANGING IN THE TREES

Bunches of cherries.

delicious!

Illustrations by Alexandra Bex   © Robert Frederick Ltd. 1998

Notes

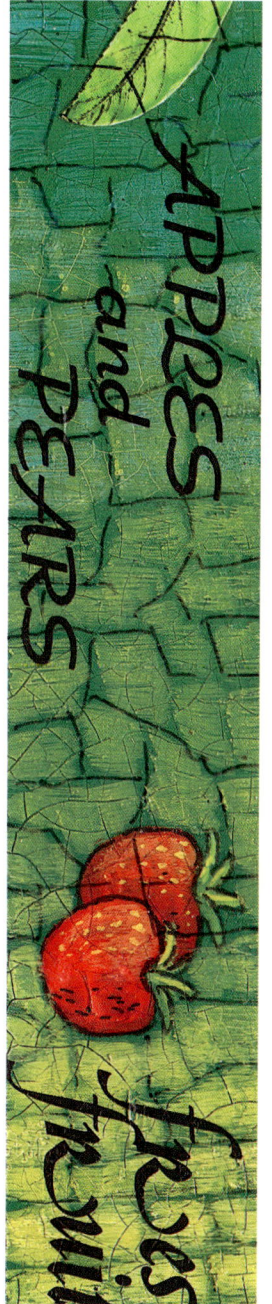

APPLES and PEARS

fruits from

Notes

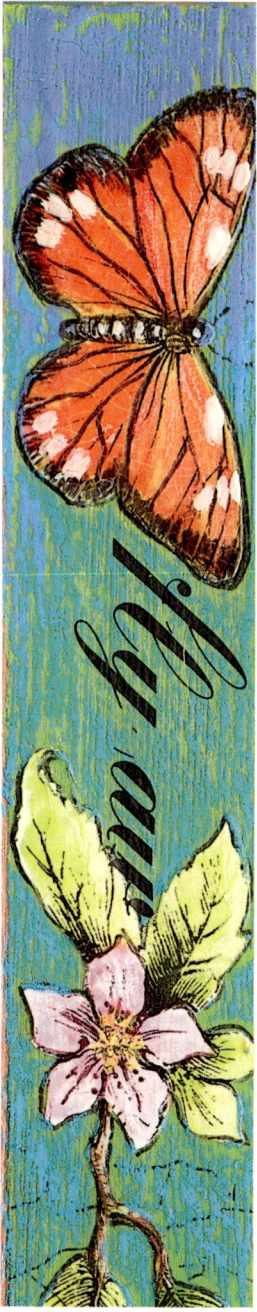

BUTTERFLY

many species fl...

Cortoiseshell and an Orange T

Illustrations by Alexandra Bex   © Robert Frederick Ltd. 1998

speckled eggs in the nest.

Notes

speckled eggs in the nest.

Notes

my black hen
lays eggs

*This is the cock that
crowed in the morn*

OCK·A·DOODLE·DOO!

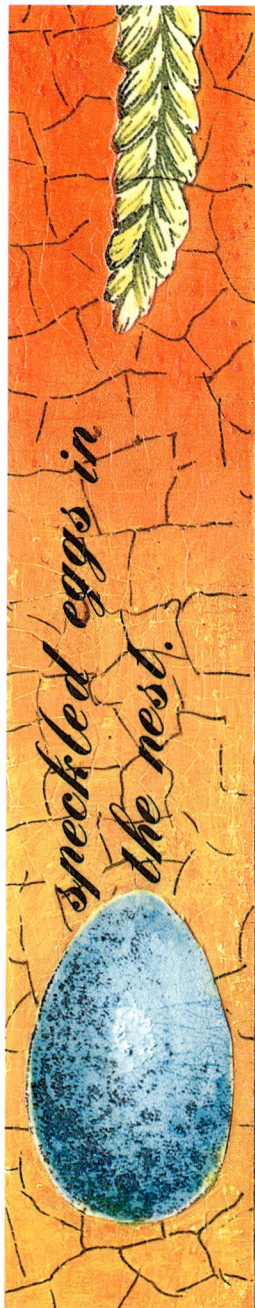

Notes

coral pink shells

Notes

coral pink shells

coral pink shells

Reflections on Water Glow

Fish and Shells to the shore

Sea Shells Cockles and I
in the sand wit

Illustrations by Alexandra Bex © Robert Frederick Ltd. 1998

LOVE

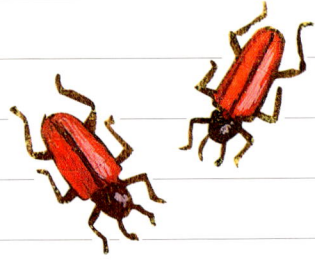

Notes

LOVE AFFAIRS bring joy and pl

I give
my
heart

My heart is like a dove...

My Love is like a red red r

Illustrations by Alexandra Bex © Robert Frederick Ltd. 1998

Notes

Notes

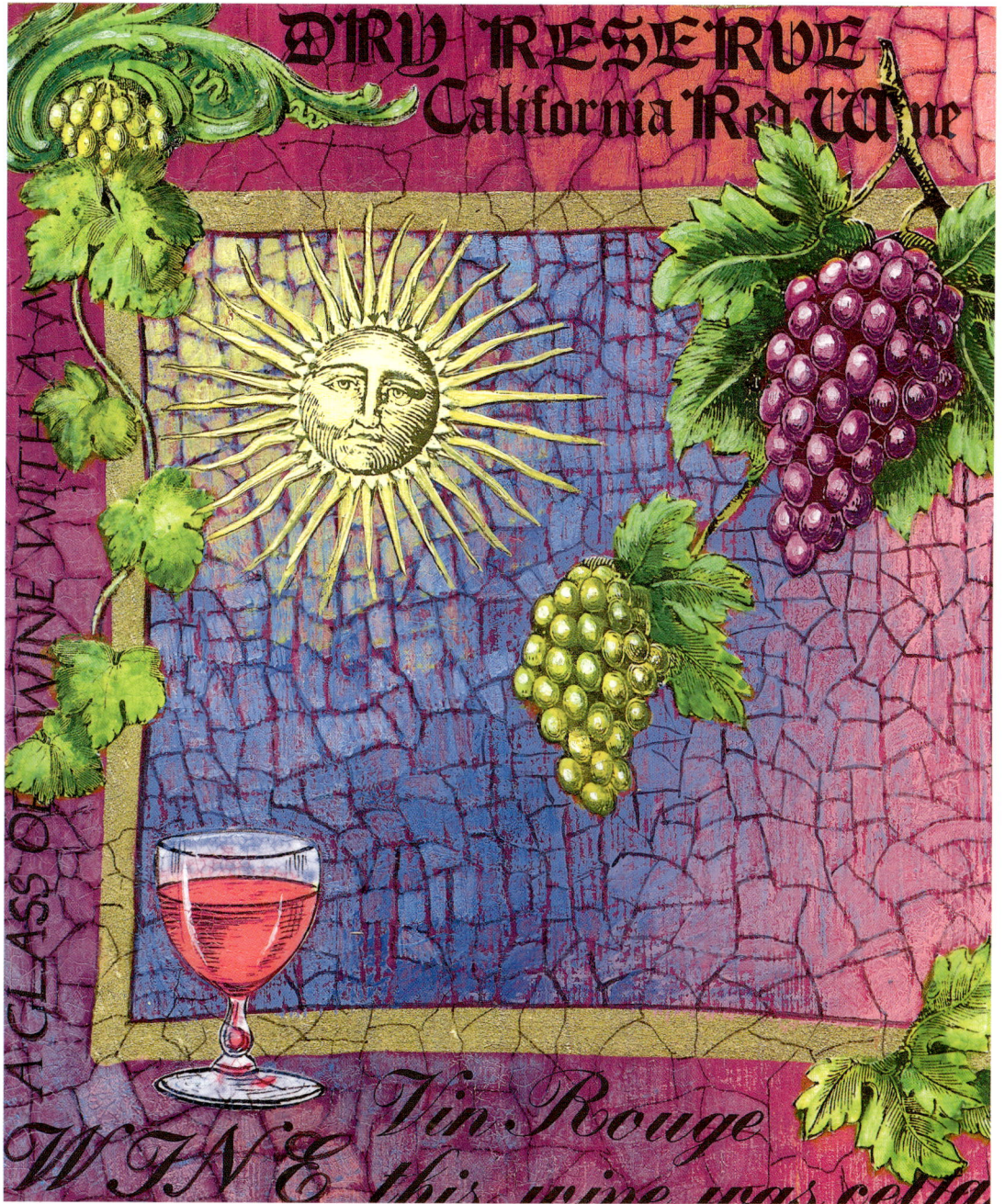

DIRY RESERVE
California Red Wine

Vin Rouge

A GLASS OF WINE WITH AY

WINE this wine was cella

Illustrations by Alexandra Bex   © Robert Frederick Ltd. 1998

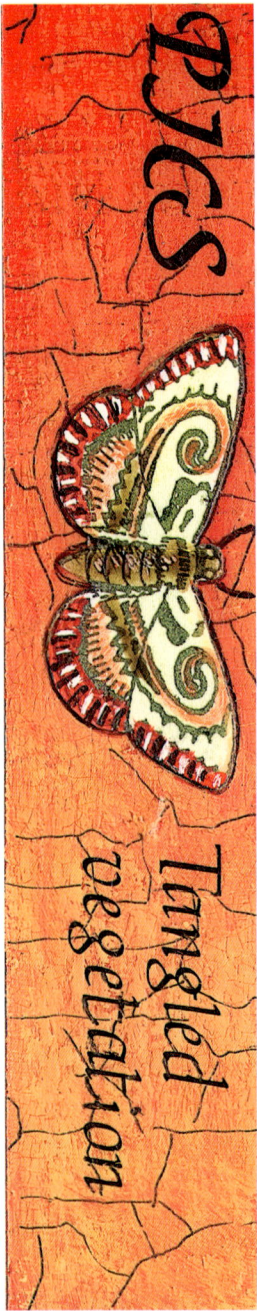

PJCS

Tangled vegetation

Notes

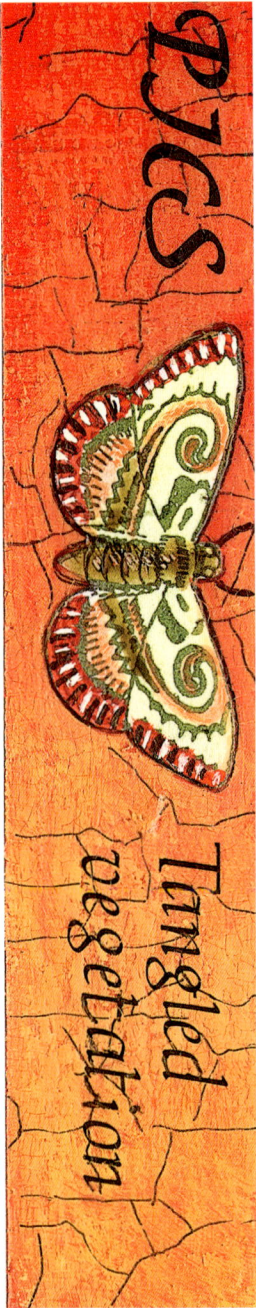

PICS

Tangled vegetation

Notes

PARROTS FLOWERS BUTTERFLIES

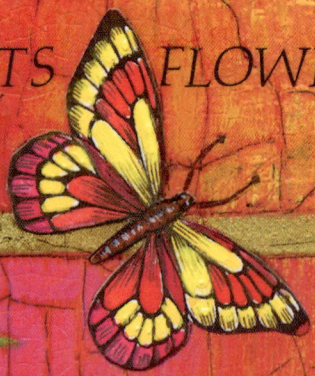

JUNGLE

vivid colours, scarlet and yellow

Notes

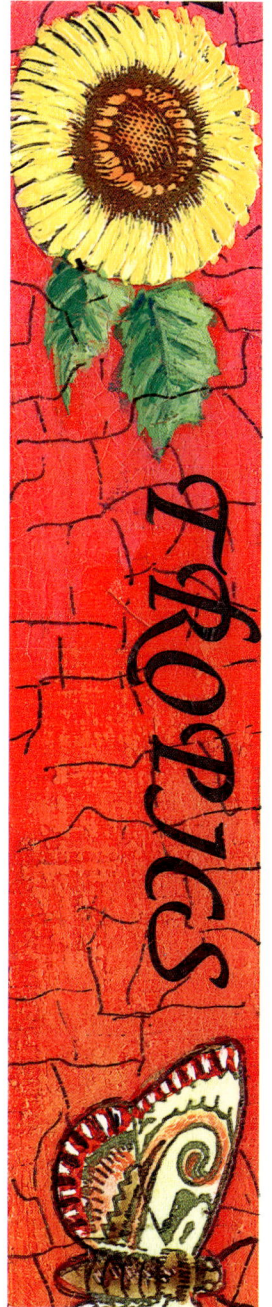

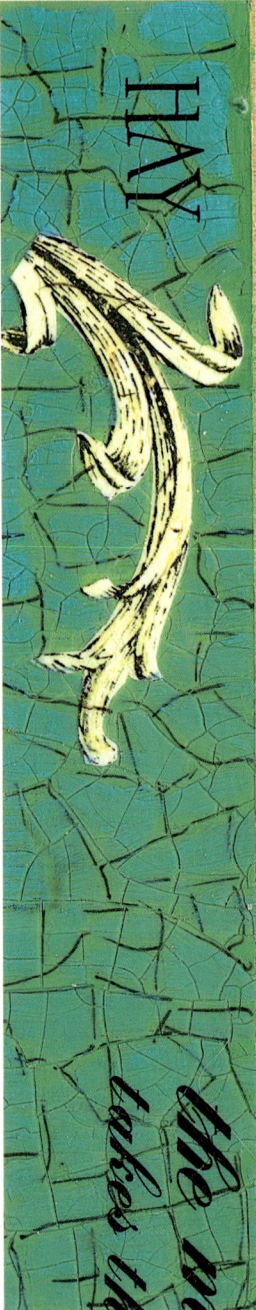

HAY

the
takes t

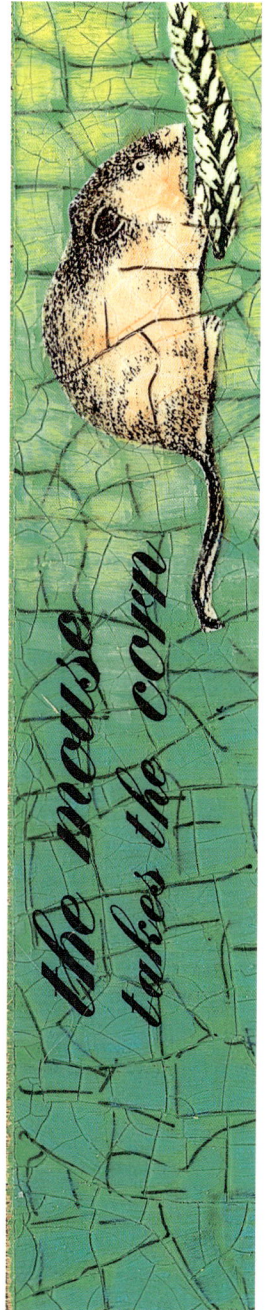

the mouse takes the corn

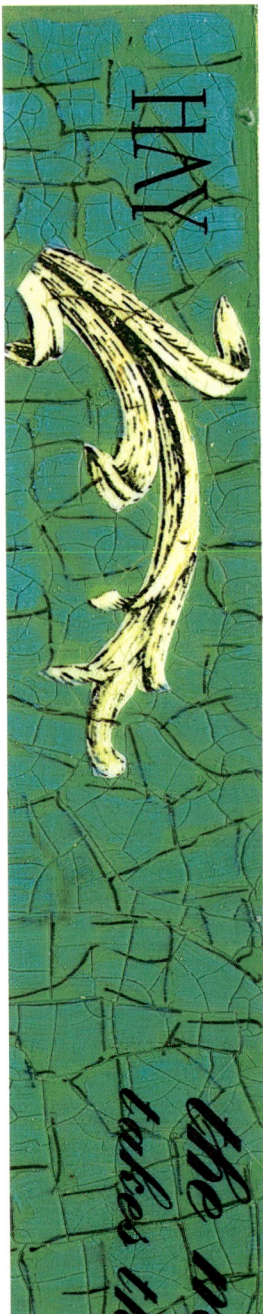

the white
dove of peace

Illustrations by Alexandra Bex © Robert Frederick Ltd. 1998

Notes

Notes

The deep blue Sea

flying fish do not actually fly

Luminous fish that light up

sea horse

starfish and coral.

Notes

Grapes

bunches of white

sweet sherry

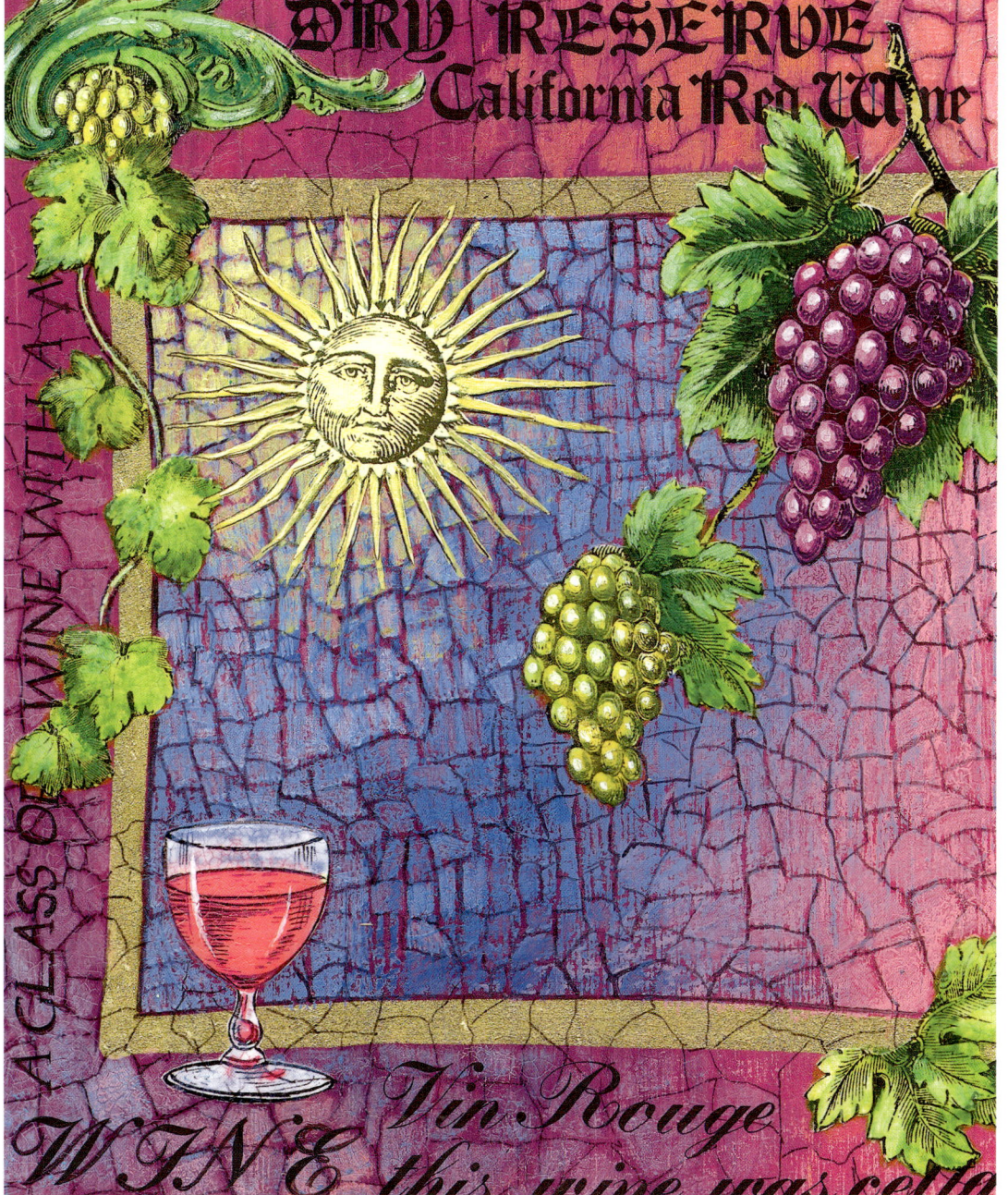

DRY RESERVE
California Red Wine

A GLASS OF WINE WITH A...

Vin Rouge
WINE this wine was cella...

Notes

Notes

my black hen
lays eggs

This is the cock that
crowed in the morn

CHICKENS ARE ROOSTING IN THE BARN

COCK·A·DOODLE·DOO!

Illustrations by Alexandra Bex   © Robert Frederick Ltd. 1998

Notes

Notes

LOVE AFFAIRS bring joy and pleasure Love is like me wild rose~briar

I give thee
my
heart

Love is like a red red rose

PJGS

Tangled vegetation

Notes

PJGS

Tangled vegetation

Notes

PARROTS FLOWERS BUTTERFLIES

JUNGLE

vivid colours, scarlet and yell

Illustrations by Alexandra Bex © Robert Frederick Ltd. 1998

Notes

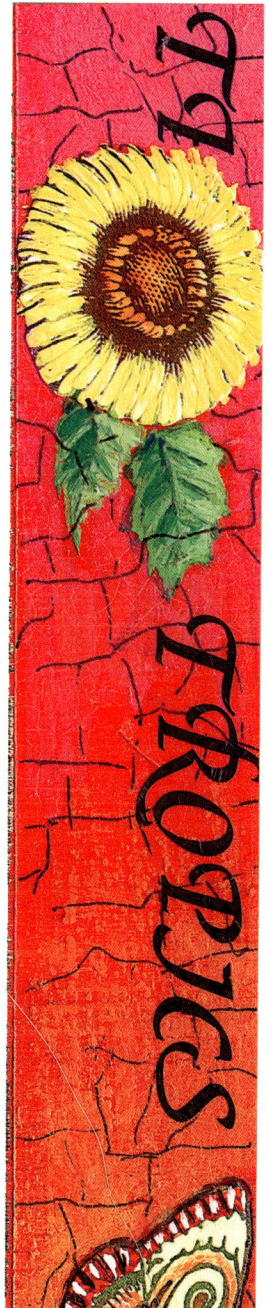

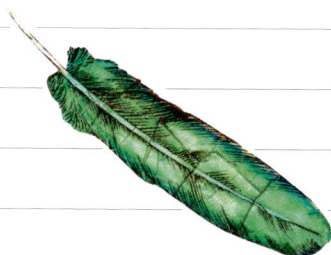

Allegro Vivace

OPERA

...usic

composed nearly fifty symphonies

Hector Berlioz

concertos & strings

If music be the food of love, play on...

Illustrations by Alexandra Bex © Robert Frederick Ltd. 1998

bunches of white

sweet sherry

Notes

bunches of whit

sweet sherry

Notes

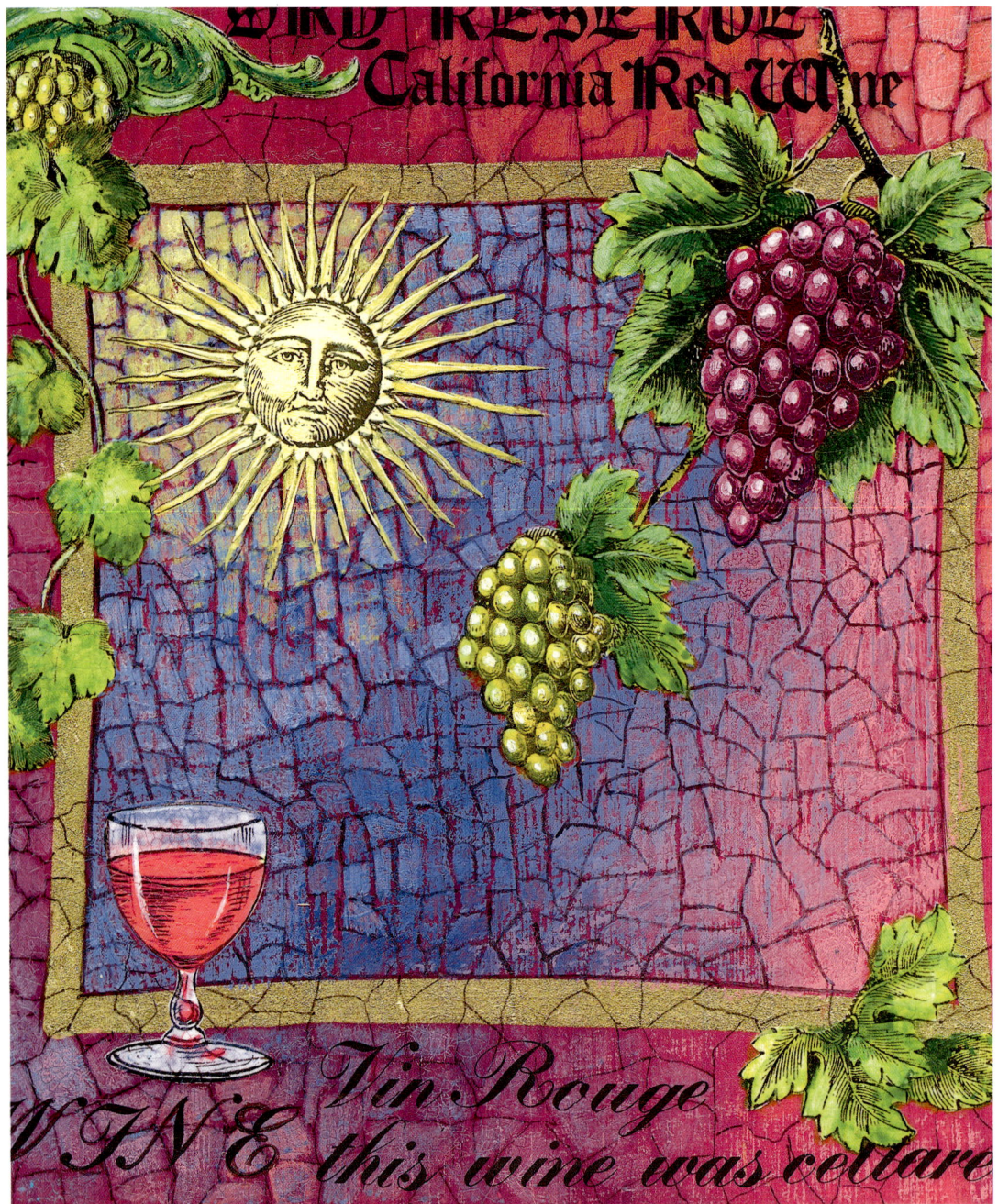

California Red Wine

Vin Rouge

WINE this wine was cellare

Illustrations by Alexandra Bex   © Robert Frederick Ltd. 1998

Notes

Notes

Notes

Notes

Tangled
vegetation

my black hen
lays eggs

CHICKENS ARE ROOSTING IN THE BARN

This is the cock that
crowed in the morn